S0-CBL-870

THE VIOLIN-MAKER'S GIFT

The Violin

Illustrated by Doug Panton

DONN KUSHNER

Maker's Gift

Macmillan of Canada • Toronto

A PEPPERMINT DESIGN

Canadian Cataloguing in Publication Data

Kushner, Donn, 1927-
The violin-maker's gift

ISBN 0-7705-1866-4

I. Panton, Doug, 1947- II. Title.

PS8571.U83V56 jC813′.54 C80-094235-3
PZ7.K87

Printed in Canada for
Macmillan of Canada
A Division of Maclean-Hunter Limited
70 Bond Street, Toronto, Ontario
Canada M5B 1X3

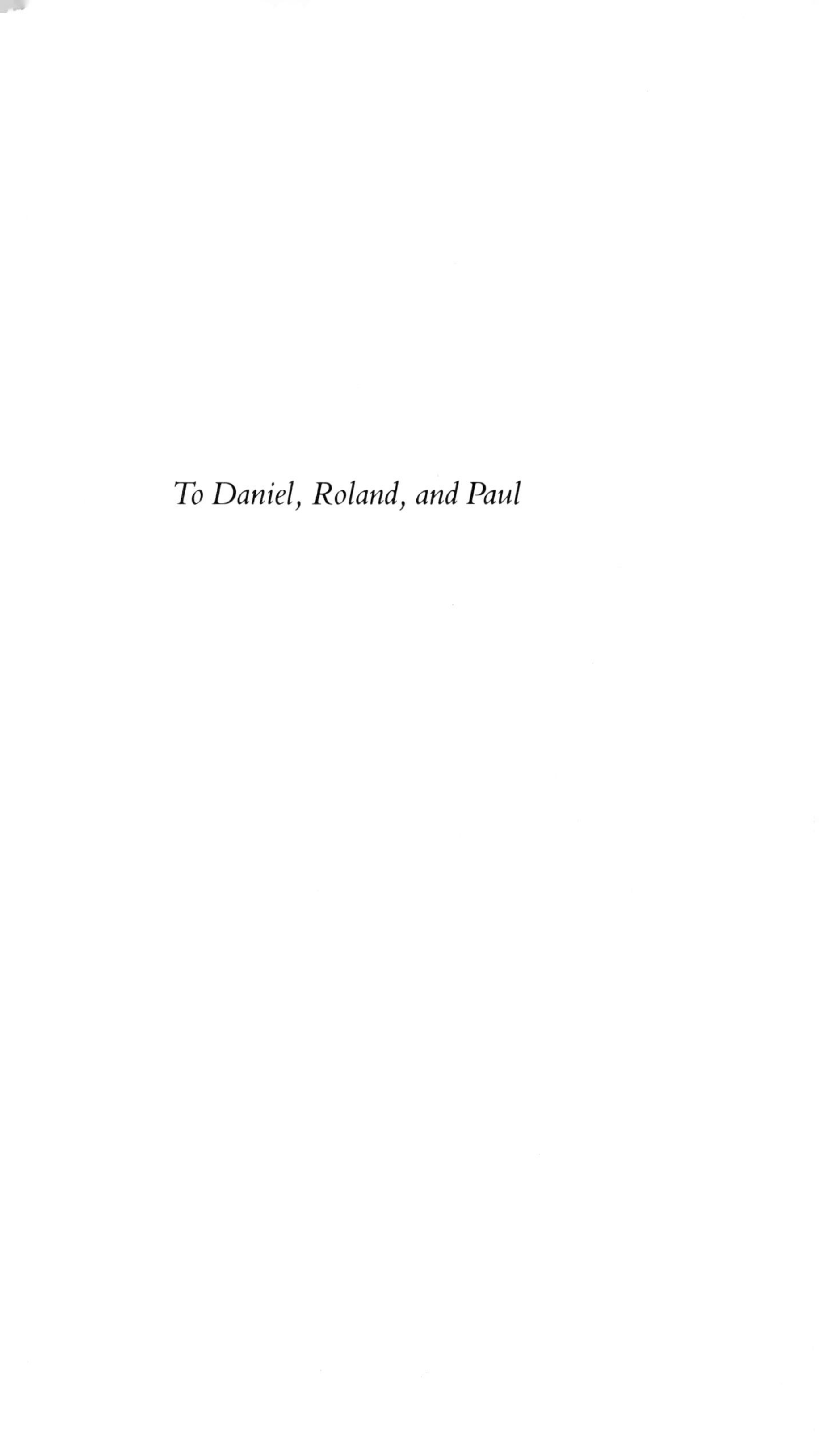

To Daniel, Roland, and Paul

BABETTE, the toll-keeper's wife, paced the corners of her look-out tower, scanning the forest below with a long brass telescope.

"Matthias!" she cried. "The warriors are coming!"

No answer came.

Babette gasped and thrust the glass to her eye again. Past a steep ravine, on the hillside where a road just showed itself now and again between low, twisted pines, a curious object appeared: a triangular rack that seemed to float along by itself, and carried a double row of new, shiny violins. Just in front of them, and a little below, a long grey donkey's head could sometimes be seen through the branches. Behind the violins a broad black hat moved along the road, and beneath the hat the red ends of a long scarf flickered in and out.

"Matthias, be on your guard! They are coming with cannons and songs. They are coming to steal your secrets and your souls. Be ready for them!"

Having given her warning twice, Babette continued her watch on the hills and forests, searching on all sides for other dangers approaching the toll gate.

But the single man approaching the toll gate under a broad hat, behind the violins and the donkey, was not leading a troop of soldiers.

Though dressed for market day—he wore a bright blue shirt in addition to the red scarf and the black hat—he was the most modest and peaceful man you could imagine. He was a very respected workman, the violin-maker Gaspard l'Innocent. At this time, before he discovered the secret that made him rich and famous, he still lived and worked in a one-room log cabin his father had left him in a forest on the northern slopes of the Pyrenees, near the Spanish border.

This was the happiest time of his life. His days were busy and quiet. Shadows and sunbeams from the tall pine forest passed over his work-bench where he sat amid the chisels, calipers, and planes and the white pieces of wood waiting to be assembled into violins. The sharp smell of varnish from violins drying on a line between the rafters mingled pleasantly with the scent of sun-warmed pine. He was never lonely. Gypsies, or travelling pedlars, or smugglers looked in as they passed; or he could always talk to Anselm, his old grey donkey, who browsed close to the cabin. Anselm's faded yellow eyes were sad and intelligent, and he seemed to understand every word that was said to him, though so far he had never answered.

In those days Gaspard's gaily varnished violins gave out a loud, clear tone. All the peasants played them at dances and weddings, and every two weeks Gaspard carried some eight of them to the little market town in the valley.

His way took him along a forest path, broad at first between the worn pine roots, then narrow and falling steeply between rows of young aspens whose branches plucked at the violin strings. Gaspard skipped from rock to rock behind the little donkey, guiding him by taps on his shoulder with an old, hairless bow.

A little after the stony path joined the dusty hillside road, Gaspard heard Babette's cry and saw her long black hair swing as she pirouetted on her tower, and the gleam of her brass telescope. He stopped for a moment, but hearing, as he expected, no sound of soldiers, continued on his way. Soon he came in sight of the arched toll bridge spanning the river, with the toll-keeper's hut beside it, clinging to the steep, rounded hillside. The squat stone tower that rose from one end of the hut might have been taken for a rocky outcrop except for the tattered tricolour flying above.

The approach to the bridge was empty, and only as Gaspard and his donkey were almost at the toll gate did a dog bark and the toll-keeper emerge from his hut. He was followed by Wagram, the great St. Bernard who had kept his feet warm nights during the terrible retreat of the Emperor Napoleon's Grande Armée from Moscow. Matthias, who had been quartermaster sergeant for the Emperor, still dressed in the remnants of his uniform. His tunic carried tattered white braid on its sleeves and the shako was still tall, though its crown was broken and the plumes had long since blown away. To the front of his shako Matthias had tied a wooden plaque on which the words "Official Toll Collector" were crudely painted in blue.

Matthias yawned and stretched.

"I thought you would be here waiting for the soldiers," Gaspard said politely. Babette called down, "Matthias! Now they are coming from the south with their drums and banners!"

The two men looked up. "She sees things that don't exist," Matthias replied. "Sometimes she imagines a rabbit is a herd of sheep, or a deer a troop of horses. But I have hardly ever heard her as excited as this—except when the Emperor died." He raised his hat. "Weeks before that news came to us she saw a long parade of black lions and elephants in the sky, with black eagles flying above them. If I were not a completely rational person, I would say some extraordinary event is about to occur. Not soldiers, necessarily; in fact probably not soldiers, but rather something very large, or possibly very small. Now, what do you have on that donkey?"

"Violins," said Gaspard patiently.

The toll-keeper repeated solemnly: "Violins." He held up one finger for silence, and reaching into the crown of his tall shako removed a folded parchment sheet of regulations, stiff with dirt and yellow with age, which, when unfolded, reached below his knees.

"'Articles on which a special tax is levied for crossing the toll bridge'," he read. "'Diamonds, rubies, emeralds'. Have you any diamonds, rubies, or emeralds?"

"No, only violins."

"'Peacocks, pearls, snapping turtles, apes, beavers, cockatoos'. Have you any cockatoos?" the toll-keeper demanded.

"No, only violins. New, shiny violins, with strong tones but no particular artistic merit, though excellent for peasant dances," Gaspard said modestly.

"Their merit does not concern me. Do you have any ammunition, fine silk, cloth of gold, soft leather purses?" The toll-keeper's eyes wandered up and down his list.

"Only violins. Please, I will be late for the fair!"

"One thing at a time!" Matthias snapped. "You have your work to do at the fair; I have my work to do here! Look at this list." He held it up and two new folds suddenly opened so that the bottom touched the ground. "These are government regulations. Do you think they were made for nothing? On certain goods a greater toll must be paid, on other ones less, on some goods no toll at all. There is no toll on

OFFICIAL
TOLL
KEEPER

the wombat, which probably does not exist; no toll on feathers or chamois skin or picture frames, though framed pictures are taxed heavily. This is why it is important for me to know exactly what you are carrying across the bridge. You seem to have a load of violins, is that correct?"

"Yes," Gaspard sighed.

"There is no tax on violins. You may pass." The toll-keeper took a brush from a little pot of whitewash that stood on one of the posts supporting the toll gate and marked a large "X" on the donkey's flank. Then he stepped back and pushed down the counterweight to raise the barrier. "Pass through quickly, please."

Only when he was far around the next bend in the road did the violin-maker remember that he had not tipped Matthias. It was the custom, even when one paid no toll, to leave a coin or a piece of fruit in passing. "He put me off with all his talk of regulations," Gaspard thought. He reflected, however, that the toll-keeper lived a lonely life. He had to pretend that his job was important and make the most of every passer-by. Then, too, it was sad for one who had been one of Napoleon's soldiers and had seen the great world to end his days as a toll-keeper on an obscure mountain road, even though his wife sometimes had visions.

"I'll find something at the market, some fine piece of fruit or a shiny trinket to make him happy when I return," Gaspard thought.

They reached the crest of the last hill. Below, the red tiled roofs of the market town clustered round the red brick belfry. In the square before the church a fountain sparkled and sprayed the pedlars' booths, roofed in blue and green cloth. Gaspard gently patted Anselm's haunches to speed him downhill and walked by his side, running his fingers over the violin strings as they descended through leafy arched plane trees that shut everything else from sight until they entered the cobbled streets of the town.

Gaspard's favourite spot was still free, on the south side of the fountain near a slim, copper-green whiskered fish that spouted water over its own back. He took four brass-tipped poles from his donkey's back and drove them into the earth to support the rack of violins. He tethered Anselm under a willow at the far side of the square and stood before his violins, calling, "Fine violins, newly made! Brighten your lives with the sound of music!" He took up one, the gayest of all—he had even gilded the ribs—and played on it: sad gypsy tunes, jolly Spanish dances, strange lullabies from the Basque country, and stirring military marches full of double-stops and flourishes. The clear, strong tone of his violin filled the square and echoed from the white façade of the Hotel de Ville to the church belfry, startling out an ever-changing spiral flight of swallows, and dying away in the open sky. Three peasant girls began to dance, at first circling him with hands joined, then whirling separately around the fountain. "Violins, fine violins!" Gaspard called. "For dances, for weddings, to still the children when they are cross, to make them sleep when they are too tired to sleep!"

"Will they really put the children to sleep?" A quiet, weary voice spoke at his elbow.

Gaspard lowered his violin. "Yes, Your Grace. People in these parts learn to play the violin very easily. Then, too, the children are used to sleeping through any amount of noise, when their families quarrel and make up, through drunken songs and the shrieking of hens being slaughtered behind the kitchen. Even if the violin is played badly, any kind of melody brings peace."

His listener, the Duke of Entrecôte, blinked his eyes sceptically. He was a tall man with an eager, lined face and a threadbare gold-laced frock-coat, who always stooped a little as he spoke. "Do you know," he said, "I have an ambition to hang violins along the great staircase in my manor house from the floor to the ceiling. Can you imagine how the light from the chandelier would fall on them? When the west wing is repaired and if the harvest is at all good, I will certainly do it. You can look for an order from me this fall."

The Duke of Entrecôte always talked this way, and at one time Gaspard had counted on making a handsome sale to him of violins whose varnish, he promised himself, would pass by subtle degrees from yellow to bright scarlet. But the Duke's estates were nearly bankrupt. He lived in style, but really more frugally than many of his tenants. He was constantly worried over money, and the most trivial mishap—a broken wagon axle or a lame goat—threw him into a state of despair worthy of a much greater sorrow.

The Duke casually picked up a violin from the rack, tuned it with the tips of his long fingers, and, taking Gaspard's bow from his hand, played a slow, melancholy Irish dance.

"You play well, Your Grace," Gaspard said.

"Passably," said the Duke. "The violin is well made." Gaspard smiled and ducked his head. "It has a strong, clear tone like all your violins but, like all of them, it lacks something. It does not sing with a human voice."

"Those are only the violins of the great masters, Your Grace," Gaspard said modestly. "Amati. Del Gesu. If I could make such violins I would not be a simple pedlar at this fair."

"You might be no better off than you are now." The Duke's tone was a little sharp. "In any case, that is not what I meant. I have heard all the great violins, of course; but however rich their tone, very few had this special quality which I have heard but once or twice in my life: as if a human soul were imprisoned in the wood, unable to leave it and only waiting to sing whenever the bow touched the strings."

"I do know what you mean," Gaspard said thoughtfully. "I played such a violin once. It was made by a little bald man with a long white beard who always looked puzzled. I asked him what his secret was—he must have had a secret because he had made several such violins: in one the voice was so clear that I could almost understand the words—but he wouldn't tell me the secret, or he had forgotten. One day when I have time I should try to discover it for myself."

"You do as well not to trouble yourself with such things." The Duke returned Gaspard's violin and bow and departed. At the far side of the square he turned to look at the rack of violins and to call, "Next time you may certainly expect a substantial order from me!"

The day passed quickly. Gaspard sold a violin to a travelling showman with a sick bear that shuffled along on four paws, head sagging to the ground. He sold one to a fat girl with long, braided hair, one to an Englishman travelling in a small go-cart, who said, "Extraordinary!" to everything he saw, and one to a frightened boy brought to the fair by his tall, stern teacher. Then he sold two to a sombre dealer from Toulouse, who took them away in a great squat black case like a coffin. It was a good day's business, and though the last sale was completed early in the afternoon he sat happily on the edge of the fountain, one eye on his remaining violins and the other on the busy market. The sunlight warmed the square, the air smelt of dust and horses and hay and roses; Gaspard stretched out his heels and leaned his head against one of the stone flowerpots that rose at intervals on the fountain's rim. The sound of falling water and the light spray touching his face made him sleepy, and he was just letting his eyelids fall when someone pulled at his sleeve.

"Look at the bird!" It was a child's voice. Gaspard was blinded at first by the sun and did not see the boy who had spoken. He turned his eyes, for relief, to the dark church portal in the shadow of the belfry, and there, on the outer fringes of the wing of a chipped limestone angel, he saw something move. The thin gypsy boy who had spoken still held his sleeve. "There he is!"

Gaspard picked his way across the square. The bird still looked like nothing but a heap of dusty feathers. It must be very young and unable to fly. Had it fallen from its nest? He could see none on the wall above. But no matter where it came from, the bird was in danger. The angel's wing was steep and worn, and the thick crowd below jostled in a ring round two gamesters who were matching a pair of coal-black fighting cocks. If the little bird should fall, it would be trampled to death, or the fierce cocks would tear it to pieces.

He noticed, without thinking of it, that bricks were missing here and there from the wall, leaving a staircase that a really agile man —not himself, of course—just might climb. He twisted and threaded through the excited crowd, raising angy murmurs as he went, and laid one hand on the wall. He looked here and there at the surface of the sun-warmed brick and became so absorbed in his study of the wall that only the gathering silence of the crowd brought him to his senses. Then he realized that he had begun to climb the wall and was already high above the ground. What an extraordinary thing to do! Should he return? A girl in the crowd below giggled. The angel was not far away; another step and he could reach it. His fingertips touched something soft, and without looking up, balancing himself somehow on a foot and a hand, he placed the bird inside his shirt. All the eyes at his back embarrassed him, and he descended the wall as he must have climbed it, his feet and hands making a way for themselves. Only when he looked up at the wall from the ground did he realize how high the angel was,

how difficult the climb must have been. The crowd had been silent through fear. What a strange way for him to act! He pulled the bird from his shirt, but it seemed in no way worth the danger he had gone through to reach it. It was quite an insignificant creature, small and brown. He would have said it was completely ordinary but for the brighter gold and blue specks he could just see among its feathers and for the golden specks in its deep-brown eyes. It looked at him, calm and fearless.

The people were looking at him, too. "That was a great treasure to risk your neck for!" said the owner of one of the game-cocks. He was putting his bird into a wicker carrying case. Its broken rival lay on the ground. "Do you plan to match it with my Pascal here?" The crowd laughed. Gaspard put the bird inside his shirt again. He felt its heart beat furiously against his skin. Then it beat more slowly and calmly. He returned to his rack of violins and sat there without calling out his wares again. The day was almost over, no one would buy now, and he could not play to attract late-comers without disturbing the little bird.

It was only when he had left the village and was in sight of the toll bridge that he asked himself seriously what he intended to do with the bird. Would he keep it? But he had no experience with such small things and no confidence that he could look after it. Once, through pity, he had taken a wounded squirrel into his hut, but it had died next day. He was afraid that the bird might slowly sicken before his eyes. He took it from his shirt and set it on a rock. Perhaps it would be kindest to let it fly away. But the bird only looked at him and hopped back and forth on one foot. Either it did not want to fly, or it was still too young. Well, he could not leave it there. It would starve or be eaten. He looked at Anselm for guidance, but the donkey, unconcerned, munched some dried poppies. Then Gaspard looked up at the toll bridge.

What an excellent idea! Perhaps the toll-keeper would like to have it. Gaspard remembered now that he had once seen a tame crow in Matthias's hut, a chipmunk in a cage, and also a weasel in a pen at the back. Matthias's attitude towards these animals was stern but kindly: Gaspard had seen him spreading a net in the river to catch fish for the weasel. The bird would surely be in good hands with the toll-keeper, and he would be able to see it from time to time. Then he remembered that in the excitement he had forgotten to bring a gift; having the bird spared him the embarrassment of facing Matthias empty-handed.

Matthias was in a relaxed and genial mood. He sat on the bridge railing resting his feet on Wagram. It was only with his dog that he departed so from his dignity, perhaps because of all they had been through together. "I see you've sold most of your violins," he called, and added graciously, "There is no tax on violins."

"Thank you," Gaspard said. "But Matthias, look at this."

"Ah." Matthias took a thoughtful step forward. "Where did you find that?"

"Oh, never mind where. It had fallen from its nest. What kind is it?"

Matthias picked the bird up. It stirred uneasily but made no attempt to escape. He looked at it carefully from all sides, even turning it over as if to decide what tax to put on it, then shook his head. "I've never seen one before. But there are so many birds. What will you do with it?"

"Why, Matthias, you see it's too small to look after itself, and I know little enough about such creatures. But it's a pretty little thing, very pretty." Gaspard pointed at the bird, still half-hidden in Matthias's hand, and saw that it was indeed pretty, that its brown eyes glowed, and that the gold tint in its feathers was stronger than he had seen at first. Perhaps he should keep it after all. But he looked at the toll-keeper's dignified, lonely face and his tongue continued, without his willing it to stop. "I thought you might like to have it."

"Ah," Matthias said.

"As pleasant company in the evenings, you know." Gaspard laughed lightly. "You might consider it as expressing my appreciation for your service here."

Matthias gnawed his lower lip and sniffed, both in and out, so that the hairs of his nostrils quivered. "Well, why not," he said finally. "It would be a shame to let it starve, since you can't look after it. I have an old cage that will do very well."

"But you'll treat it well, Matthias?" The toll-keeper sniffed again and turned away. This did not worry Gaspard. He knew that Matthias was often brusque in accepting gifts, as if someone might suspect him, a man of absolute integrity, of taking bribes. As the violin-maker walked away, he tried to picture the last expression he had seen in the little bird's eyes. Was it a look of reproach at being abandoned, of bewilderment at finding itself in the toll-keeper's great paw, or of gratitude at being left in such safe hands? Gaspard did not know which he wanted to believe. He was so absent-minded as he walked along that Anselm had to seize his sleeve in his teeth to keep him on the path. That evening, after dark, Gaspard returned alone to the toll-keeper's hut.

Matthias had installed the bird very comfortably in a roomy wicker cage. The floor was padded with crumpled dry rushes, and the bird had made itself a cozy hole in one corner of these. Only its head showed. It had fed well from a dish of boiled wheat. "So that's all that's needed," Gaspard thought. He was still standing just inside the doorway. The toll-keeper, who never actually welcomed people inside his hut, stood between him and the cage as if in a moment he would tell him to go.

"I thought, perhaps, I might look after the little bird myself after all, if you don't mind," said Gaspard.

The toll-keeper was silent for a full half-minute. "Ah, the little bird," he said. "Certainly there are many little birds in the world if one knows where to look; it isn't necessary to climb church steeples to find them." Others from the fair had crossed the bridge after he, Gaspard realized. "You may say that little birds are common enough, so that I could always find another, or you could find one for me. And you might also say that it was you who found the creature, you who rescued it. But you carried it in your shirt where it would have suffocated, or your donkey might have eaten it"—he held up his finger at Gaspard's startled protest—"whereas I only fed it and kept it warm. Who is to judge between us?"

"But if there are so many birds to be found, Matthias!"

"Any number! More than you realize! But remember, you did not leave the bird with me only for safekeeping: it was a token of appreciation of my services. If you took it away now I would have to conclude that you do not appreciate my services. Have you brought another gift to replace this one?"

How foolish not to have thought of that! Gaspard was silent while the toll-keeper laid a dark cloth over the cage. "On my next trip, Matthias," he pleaded.

"By all means," Matthias said unsympathetically, opening the door for Gaspard's departure. "Whenever you come."

Only then did Gaspard realize that Babette was also in the room, sitting quietly in the corner, a thing he had never seen her do before. As he walked out the door, Babette began to sing an old cradle song in a low, sweet voice.

Gaspard planned to return next morning, but it rained that night and the wind lifted ten shingles from the roof: he had to spend all day repairing it. The next day he made a wreath of needles and pine cones; he varnished the needles so that they would always stay green and gilded the cones. But the paint did not dry until morning. He decided to take advantage of the sunlight for the fine work of fitting together the backs of four violins, and so he arrived at the toll-keeper's hut only after dark, supporting the wreath carefully on a forked stick.

"Very pretty," Matthias said, "though with your skill I'm sure you could make a dozen like that in a day. But I value the bird you gave me a little more. Look at it."

The bird was larger now and quite firm on its legs. It walked up and down the cage proudly and hopped jauntily to the perch. "It doesn't sing yet," Matthias said, "but just see its feathers. They only appeared this morning."

A ring of scarlet feathers now circled the bird's neck, a deep, rich scarlet interspersed with black. The hints of gold in the feathers had developed. Faint gold bands now appeared on the outside of its wings, and the underside of the wings and throat were snowy white. "Oh, no," Matthias said, "this is not a bird to exchange for a pretty wreath. You yourself will agree that it is worth more. Perhaps one of your violins. I have often felt that I too could play the violin if I tried."

"A violin in exchange for a little bird! You must be mad, Matthias!" Gaspard left, forgetting his wreath.

He returned a week later with a fine new violin. He had painted butterflies on its back and hummingbirds on its ribs and he carried it in a case of walnut, lined with chamois skin.

Matthias stroked the strings with his great, blunt fingers. "Now, that is a real gift," he said, half sadly. "I could almost wish you had brought it before I realized the true value of the bird you gave me."

The bird, now grown too large for the cage, sat on a perch before the window, tethered by a thin brass chain. The gold bars on its wings had spread, and their colours were so intense that the wings seemed to be encased in a living network of metal. It was a male. From the top of its head very fine golden feathers rose to a shimmering crest. The scarlet band around its throad now spread over its shoulders like a cape, and scarlet feathers encased its legs. Its claws and beak seemed made of gold blended with rubies. Gaspard thought that only the expression in its dark eyes was still the same.

"I always dreamed of finding a treasure," Matthias said in a low, solemn voice, "but I never knew how it would come. I thought I might have the chance of doing a rich man a favour, say of mending his wagon if it happened to break down near my door; or I might follow the gypsies into the forest when they bury their gold—but that would be dangerous. Just to think that a simple act of kindness on my part, in taking the little bird off your hands, should have turned out so well! It shows that one should never hesitate too long before doing an unselfish deed—some benefit may come from it."

Matthias rubbed his hands and went on to describe his plans for the bird. He had considered selling it to a zoo—though he had to admit he had grown fond of it—but then he had decided, shrewdly, that there was more profit in keeping the bird and putting it on display. "Even as he is now he's worth twenty centimes to look at, wouldn't you say?" He would build a new cage, big enough for the bird to move in freely, but with close bars to prevent the peasants from reaching in to pluck the golden feathers.

There was still the problem of where to put this cage. Babette was too occupied with other things to tend the bridge. He could not very well leave his job to travel around the fairs, and he did not like to show the cage inside the hut, for that was government property, and there might be some regulation against its use for displaying birds. He thought he would build a little curtained booth just off the road, a few steps from his hut, so that he could show the bird to the public while keeping an eye on his other business. He would, of course, keep the financial records for the bird completely separate from those concerned with the collection of tolls.

CHAPTER TWO

GASPARD packed his violin in its case, picked up his wreath, and returned to his hut. For the next month, though he went to market each week, more often than ever before, he refrained from asking Matthias questions about the bird or from looking into the hut. After he had passed the hut twice he found this easy. However, news of "Matthias's wonderful bird" reached him in scraps and dribbles. People talked of it at the fair; beggars at his door brought him stories of the bird in exchange for bread and cheese; the wandering mushroom-pickers chatted about it to each other in their strange accents as they searched, basket in hand, among the needles in the shadows of his pine forest.

The bird continued to grow until its wings spanned about three feet—some said five, but Gaspard believed the lower figure—then stopped. The gold bands on the wings looked so solid that the peasants were sure that when the bird moulted the falling feathers would ring like coins. The crest of golden feathers on his head had grown to a comb that shone like wheat in the autumn sun. He still did not sing, but began to emit cooing sounds, high and low, mixed with guttural clucks and strange chirps.

Then, one day the bird began to speak. This marvel was reported to Gaspard with such excitement and in such conflicting detail that at first he was ready to discount it completely, as he had learnt to disbelieve so many of the miraculous stories he heard.

For people in these parts saw strange things, though none so many as Babette, who was sometimes called "Mad Babette". Some families had seen the Three Kings tramping up and down the snowy slopes, guided only by the light of a quarter-moon, searching in vain among the rocks and spruce trees for the Child. An ancient, half-blind farmer who lived quite alone swore that every Easter Eve Judas himself poked and rattled through the straw and rusty ploughs and decayed harness of his barn for a sound rope. One never knew whether to believe such visions, though the people who saw them did not know enough to lie; and it was agreed that even if they were true, they were true only for these people. But too many stories of the talking bird were told to dismiss them, even though they conflicted wildly. Some said the bird had started talking immediately, others that it had developed a vocabulary little by little, like a child, though in a period of days rather than years. All agreed that its command of language was extraordinary, that it knew words like "heather", "academy", "semiquaver", "estuary", "bill-of-lading", and "deciduous". According to some reports it knew things that no one could have taught it: the names of side streets in villages fifty miles away, of flowers that bloomed only on the other side of the mountains, of battles in which the grandfathers of the oldest peasants had taken part a hundred years before.

Others swore that the bird was only a mimic, though much cleverer than any parrot, and could only repeat exactly what it had heard. They assured Gaspard that it had done nothing but say their own words again in a strident, mocking voice. People also disagreed about the bird's accent. According to one old woman, travelling through the forest on a pilgrimage to the sea-shore, it spoke exactly like a Spanish grandee she had heard in her youth; her middle-aged daughter who accompanied her stayed behind a moment to whisper to Gaspard that her mother was mistaken and that the bird had an unmistakable Basque accent. By some the bird was said to speak like a Parisian gentleman, by others like a Breton or even like an Englishman taught French by the monks. In the past Gaspard would have gone himself to find out the truth among all these tales but now he said to anyone who asked him that he could not leave his work for such a trivial reason.

CHAPTER THREE

IN EARLY AUTUMN, when the leaves had turned their ripest colours, Gaspard crossed the toll bridge again. The little river chased itself beneath a canopy of white and gold birches; under the bridge it ran between buttresses of white granite, sparkling with mica. Golden leaves covered the grey stone bridge and the road. A dozen farmers stood in line at the entrance to the booth, a hut of worn and stained canvas on a framework of spruce saplings, and another dozen pairs of feet could be seen inside in the gap between the canvas and the ground. Gaspard and his donkey had to pick their way through a flock of sheep that a vacant-eyed farmer's boy had herded into the middle of the road while his master visited the booth. Above the entrance a green sign said in dripping red letters, "Matthias's Wonderful Bird". By looking more closely Gaspard could see that the words "Matthias's Fantastic Bird" had first been painted there and had not been completely covered by a second coat of green paint.

Matthias came running out of the booth. "No tax on violins!" he panted. Then, when he had caught his breath, he added, "Some people think that because I have two occupations they can get by me. You have no idea what they have tried to smuggle past here in the last month. I catch them every time! Look." He pointed proudly at an iron-barred shed at the side of his hut. Gaspard saw rolls of silk stacked like firewood, and strings of amber beads hanging from pegs, a tooled leather saddle with silver stirrups in one corner, and a sad-eyed fox. "All confiscated," Matthias said proudly. "They don't get in to see the bird without paying, either, no matter how busy I am at the bridge. Wagram is on guard." At the sound of his name, the great St. Bernard, lying near the door of the booth, lifted his muzzle from the dirt and cocked one ear. Gaspard heard a sudden silence as the murmuring within the booth died, and then a high, clear voice, sweet as rain falling through maple leaves, sang:

Sow your seed in the early morning,
Pass the tavern before the light,
Do not forget the sun is shining.

Another will gather your crops in the evening
And shut the tavern door at night,
But do not forget the sun is shining.

A second silence followed this strange song. Gaspard looked questioningly at the toll-keeper. "Oh, for you there's no charge of course!" said Matthias generously. "You can walk right in!"

"No," Gaspard said, "I must be getting on to the fair."

Matthias sniffed. "Well, if your business is so important. But the price may be higher next time." Gaspard nodded and continued on his way. He returned from the village after dark when the booth was shut, and the toll-keeper, hearing the familiar sound of Anselm's hooves, called out in a sleepy voice, "Pass on, pass on, no tax on violins."

CHAPTER FOUR

NOW GASPARD began to work harder than ever. The lines of drying violins overflowed his cabin and hung like gourds in a shed he built outside the back door. He got up in time to catch the first morning light and worked until his fingers stiffened in the chilly dusk. But he still refused to work by lamplight and his violins were as carefully made as ever—and as undistinguished. Many of them still exist, signed with a "G. l'I." at the base of the neck, followed by a tiny pine cone. They often turn up in pawnshops and in the shops of small dealers, where any expert customer will wrinkle his nose and declare, incorrectly, that such an open, almost blatant tone could never have come from the hands of Gaspard l'Innocent.

Gaspard arranged to sell six violins a month to the dealer from Toulouse. Thus, he often found it possible to avoid the fair in the market town. When he did go, he still played his violins and still called to the crowd to buy them, but at regular intervals, and the town's three drunkards, who sunned themselves by the corner of the church, complained of this regularity. Formerly it had been pleasant to doze, never knowing when music would enter their dreams, but now Gaspard played for half an hour in the morning, then quietly at noon, so as not to disturb the market women's babies sleeping at the back of the booths, and then for a third time before he left in the evening. Thus, he told himself, he was keeping up all aspects of his trade.

People still talked of his climb, and many claimed to have seen it. They described it in such detail that, to believe them, Gaspard must have been agile as a fly and fearless as a monkey. Everyone also assumed that he had sold the bird to Matthias for a handsome price. He denied this at first, but his words met with such sceptical looks, such whistling and winking, that he soon gave up. To Gaspard's disappointment, even the Duke of Entrecôte congratulated him on the great profit he had made through his heroic act. But then, the Duke could be forgiven if all his thoughts turned towards money. His affairs were going very badly. He had been forced to take in the family of his wife's second cousin—a gouty, ignorant haberdasher—as paying guests, and though they still addressed him as "My Lord", he had become little more than a steward to them. Now his only thoughts were of ways in which he could somehow escape his load of debts, and every day he evolved a hundred fanciful schemes which he was too sensible to try.

To all the compliments and inquiries he received, Gaspard answered as little as possible. Many thought him overly modest, or even dull, but some were convinced that he was really very sly and that he had secretly retained an interest in the talking bird. It was these who gave him the most information about the bird, half ironically, as if to have their statements confirmed; and it was from one of them, a tall, leathery straw-and-feed merchant, that Gaspard first learned that the bird could predict the future.

"It happened this way," the merchant said solemnly. "I was standing there listening to it. It costs fifty centimes, but I consider it money well spent, for who knows when I'll see a talking bird again? It was answering old riddles that Mère Pèlerine was asking it. She knows a thousand of them, but she's forgotten all the answers. You know, 'Why is a mouse unlike a sheaf of wheat, except in the winter?' and 'If six grains of barley are left in the bottom of an empty sack, which is the wisest?' This led me to think of some unsold sacks of oats at the back of my warehouse, three years old now and dried out. No one would buy them, I was sure, and I had decided to clear the space by giving them to my wife's spotted pigs, Pierrot and Colombine. Then the bird looked at me directly and said, 'Wait, something else will happen.' Then it was silent again for the rest of the evening. Nothing could tempt it to speak again: corn, coins, sugar cubes dipped in cognac. However, I believed its advice was meant for me and I did wait, and sure enough before three days had passed a sausage manufacturer bought my sacks of oats: for feeding *his* pigs, he said, but I suspect he mixes flour with his sausage meat. Isn't that wonderful?"

Gaspard did not think so. He found the story banal and sordid and thought it very unlikely that the bird he had rescued at such peril would have anything to say to a greasy-souled merchant. But he heard more stories: the bird told Mère Naufrage, whose three sons had been lost at sea, that two of them had been rescued. Sure enough, that very evening the younger son knocked at the door and led his trembling mother back to the tavern where the oldest brother had stopped to drink to the soul of the lost one and to his own safe delivery.

The bird spoke up and told the miserly farmer Crevette that a ten-franc piece he had lost would be found under the dirt of the henyard. Crevette found it at dawn, after a night of digging, and just in time, too. He had sworn that if the sun rose before the coin was found he would disinherit his son, whom he suspected of stealing it, and drive him and his family from the house.

The bird also told the wealthy widow Latulippe that the new singing teacher with long black mustaches and soulful eyes, whom she had brought at great expense from Italy, would advise her to abandon her dreams of fame on the concert stage and would return home, taking her parlour-maid with him. Sometimes the bird predicted good events, sometimes bad, sometimes important ones and sometimes trivial, but it always told the truth, and its fame spread.

CHAPTER FIVE

GASPARD crossed the toll bridge again on a late autumn day, when the dry yellow leaves were trodden into the ground and the bare, dead-white branches rubbed and chattered together in the wind. A dense green cloud looked over the opposite hill from a grey sky. Three carriages waited before the booth, almost blocking the road. As Gaspard and his donkey passed the last in line, the driver, a great broad-hatted Slovak with mustaches hanging beneath his chin, leaned over tipsily and tried to flick the strings of the violins with the amber stem of his long pipe. Next came a high phaeton, glistening with brass and new leather, and bearing on the door a blue and white coat of arms, two sea-lions on an ice-floe. Two English grooms sat stiffly on it in their scarlet coats, never turning their heads. First in line was an open farm cart, whose driver sat asleep, covered to his ears with a great plaid blanket half of which also covered the hindquarters of his horse. In the back of the cart the Duke of Entrecôte sat, briskly rubbing his hands together under his faded yellow cloak.

"So your bird has made his name in the capitals of the world," he said to Gaspard.

"He isn't my bird, Your Grace."

"The Count Cerné Vary came all the way from Prague to consult your bird on a matter of high finance. I've learned this from his coachman." The Duke pointed over his shoulder to the drunken Slovak, who had now put his great boots on his horse's back and was trying to flick dust from their toes with his whip without hitting the horse; but his aim was bad, and at almost every stroke the horse started forward, jolting the English carriage, whose grooms jerked stiffly forward and back but did not turn their heads. "The Count talks in his sleep," the Duke said, "and his coachman tells me he stands to make or lose a fortune, depending on the grape harvest in the Rhineland. The Earl of Fressingborough is bothered by a more domestic problem. Her ladyship expects a child within the month, and the Earl cannot wait to know if it will be a boy at last, or a girl like the other six. He was so eager to get here that his grooms had to restrain him from hiring a horse at the last inn and riding ahead. Only the thought of his own dignity stopped him, and even so, he came in his slippers." The Duke sniffed and wiped his nose on a great cambric handkerchief that he then thrust back into his coat sleeve.

"Now, I am here on a matter of some moment too, I can tell you, though no one else

must know. I have an offer for my olive grove beyond the old mill. A good offer—never mind how much—but such a one won't come again soon. It was made by a newly rich manufacturer of fishhooks, who has picked up the idea that only an olive grove on an old stony hillside can really express the importance of his position. He insists on the stones; I think he cares more for them than for the trees. But the loss of the grove would cut my estate almost in half, and this sale sticks in my throat. My great-aunt is past ninety now, and her mind is wandering. She imagines herself young again and surrounded by admirers; for she was once the sweetheart of all the court, you know, and narrowly escaped with her head and fortune after the Revolution. I believe that I am her chief heir and that she will not live long. The bird can tell me. I will grieve for my aunt sincerely"—the Duke turned on Gaspard a completely honest look—"but she is enough like me to agree, if she could, that the land must be preserved above all. If my aunt dies in time I will keep my olive grove and all its rocks."

Gaspard nodded sympathetically. "I hope the bird gives you the answer you want, Your Grace."

"I hope so indeed; but I would be glad to hear of my great-aunt's recovery, too. To think that having lived so long she can now only dream of the baubles of this world! But the bird might not answer me, you know. Sometimes he refuses to answer. We only know that he speaks truly about the future if he speaks at all. Will you come in with me? I am sure he would speak to you."

"No, no," Gaspard said quickly, "I must go to the fair." He pressed his donkey forward. He felt the Duke's look of reproach and bent his head.

"There is no tax on violins." The voice that greeted Gaspard at the bridge was that of a tall, stout young man with sleepy eyes and hairy ears, who pushed down the counterweight of the barrier with as great an effort as if it weighed as much as the bridge itself.

"Where is Matthias?"

"I am Matthias's second cousin." With the barrier up at last, the young man seemed in no hurry to let it fall. "Now that there is work for two, he sent for me to teach me his trade. He has even said that if the work with the bird increases—if, for example, he acquires another one—I will be promoted to showman, and *my* second cousin can take my place here."

"There can never be another such bird," Gaspard said. When he was well past the bridge, just before the bare trees finally hid it from sight, he looked back and saw that the cousin was still waving cheerfully at him with one hand, and was still leaning on the counter-weight; the pole of the barrier quivered, and it too waved at Gaspard.

CHAPTER SIX

AT THE BEGINNING of winter Matthias closed the booth by his hut, left the toll bridge in the charge of his cousin, and began to travel around the countryside showing his bird to the public. Babette, who had become skilled at caring for the bird, came with him. She had become quieter, as if she were less in need of the company of visions.

Despite his good nature, the cousin learned the rules of the bridge well and enforced them as strictly as Matthias, though with less delay. When Gaspard passed the bridge now the light booth opposite the hut winked at him mockingly with its torn, flapping canvas. The cousin told him all the news of Matthias, where his travels had taken him, the crowds that came to see the bird, and its owner's great prospects. He spoke of opera houses with velvet curtains, of concert halls with glittering pillars, and of the grand ballrooms of fashionable hotels, but he was never sure of exact names. All the violin-maker could really learn was that Matthias had travelled as far east as Perpignan and as far north as the outskirts of Toulouse, but no farther. This surprised Gaspard, who had expected that the bird would carry its owner in splendour to Paris, if not to all the capitals of the world, as far away to him as the stars. One cold spring day he learned that the toll-keeper was exhibiting the bird at the Golden Snail, an inn at the outskirts of his own market town.

Years ago Gaspard had visited this inn. It was small and hidden away in twisting alleyways, too far from the main roads to serve the carriages of the rich. Its name stirred up memories of discomfort and failure, of petty criminals and dishonest commercial travellers, all the shady, homeless folk who avoid the light but have to eat and sleep somewhere. It seemed farther away from royal capitals and gay courts than Gaspard himself. He decided that this time he would look at the bird again.

The inn was even shabbier than he remembered it. It huddled at the end of a blind alley, away from the light, between the high blank walls of warehouses. The cobbles before it were covered with mud and straw from the row of farm carts that half blocked the inn door. In the narrow space between the carts and the wall a crowd of restless farmers passed to and fro. Boys sat on the wagon wheels calling to their dogs, who chased each other through the feet of the crowd. On one cart a gypsy strummed a stained guitar and sang about the hardships of a soldier's life. The sun was setting, and the snow that had melted during the day was beginning to freeze again. The upper reaches of the warehouse wall glowed a mottled purple. At the corner of the alley beggars sat around a fire, feeding it with scraps of an old mattress.

Gaspard edged forward through the crowd which became thicker as he came closer to the door: at the end he had to push through a group shuffling in the corridor, unwilling either to pay to enter or to leave. Gaspard dropped twenty centimes into a box guarded by the dour innkeeper and picked his way to the last empty space, a clearing behind one of the pillars supporting the low ceiling of the long, dim room. By craning his head and standing on tiptoe he could just see an empty trestle table lit by four smoky lanterns suspended from poles at the corner. Smoke also rose in the air from a hundred pipes and from the fireplace at the far end of the room which was choked with wet wood. Gaspard coughed. The air would be very bad for the bird. He wondered how often it was forced to perform in such rooms. Elbows thrust into his ribs, and somehow more people pushed in front of him. He was shoved back toward the wall until he could go no farther. His back was pressed against a wet sack that seemed filled with sticks of firewood.

He felt a tap on his shoulder. "So you have

come at last," the Duke of Entrecôte said. Even here, the Duke had room to himself, for the crowd had made a little clearing around him in respect for his fine new coat. It was yellow, with bright silver buttons, and its skirts fell almost to the ground. Below them Gaspard could see the shining buckles of the Duke's new shoes.

"Your Grace has been in luck. Did the bird bring it? Did your great-aunt die?"

"No, and no. The luck came by itself. Still, I might not have waited for it if I had not thought the bird would help me somehow—though in fact it told me nothing. But surprisingly, my great-aunt recovered from her illness and her mind became active again. But she lost something of her old spirit, burnt her fine clothes, broke her mirrors, covered her gay wallpaper with heavy green drapes, set her pedigreed spaniels free, and walled up her jewels. She also gave away many things, and I received five cases of old coins, which she said I could drown if I chose. But to my amazement I was able to sell them for the price of five farms. Now I am comfortable again. I have paid my debts, and packed my cousin and his family away. They have gone to a hotel on the coast where, I hear, the sea air torments his gout. I have restored my cattle-yard and bought myself this coat."

"It is very becoming, Your Grace."

"Thank you." The Duke added modestly, "It looks best with the hat"—he lifted a wide white-plumed hat from the level of his waist—"but that would block the view of the people at my side. But here comes the bird."

From the door at the far corner of the room a cage emerged and edged forward through the slowly parting crowd. It walked on a pair of sturdy legs in black trousers, and two black arms, with white gloves, grasped it from behind. The cage was so large that only when Matthias set it on the table and stepped back could his face be seen. He was wearing a showman's top hat which the cage had pushed to the back of his head, and he wiped his sweaty face with a silk handkerchief that he then returned to the tail pocket of his coat, making an odd bulge. When he stepped away from the cage it could be seen that Babette had walked in behind him. She too wore a top hat, shorter than her husband's; a snare drum hung from her shoulder, and two red drumsticks were poised in her hands. Matthias reached inside the cage and took out the bird, holding it carefully until he had fastened a light chain from the cage to a ring on its leg. The bird was bunched together at first, a round ball of feathers from which a slim neck and a head stuck out. He stepped from foot to foot and shook out his wings. Light shone from his golden beak and comb, dimly through the smoky air. Gaspard could see the crest and the wings, the red legs and the gold feet, but dully, like a bad portrait or a fish seen through muddy water.

"Now, here is my famous bird," Matthias said in a hoarse voice, still panting a little. Babette started to stroke her drum and a faint rustling began over which Matthias's voice rose more strongly: "You've all heard of him, otherwise you wouldn't be found in such a stuffy place—except you, Père Fidèle," he added to a small man, cracked like a withered gourd, who hugged his knees by the chimney corner. "You're always in the tavern, everyone knows that. But the rest of you are here to hear my bird foretell the future, perhaps to have your own future foretold. My bird can tell you everything, past and future both, if he chooses!" Matthias looked angrily round the crowd, and the bird half opened one wing. The wings had certainly grown, Gaspard thought. This one spanned the table. How cramped the bird must feel in its cage!

"Who will be the first to ask?" Matthias demanded. "Only a franc for the right to ask my bird a question!"

"Why so little?" Gaspard whispered.

"Because he may not answer," the Duke

said. "Matthias would soon become rich if he could discover how to make the bird speak each time, since, as he says, it always speaks the truth. But it is risking money, and these people are stingy. A franc is as much as they can bear to lose without cursing and throwing things. Matthias is not afraid for himself but for the bird."

"But why in an inn? Why in such low company?"

"Only a franc!" Matthias called. "Who will give? Are you afraid to know the truth?"

A gaunt peasant woman, her face hidden by a long blue handkerchief, strode forward, slapped a franc on the bare wooden table, and cried accusingly, "Will my cow never calve?"

A squat, gangling simpleton ambled up just behind her. His feet were spread like a duck's and his round eyes goggled. He laid his franc gently on the table, and gently said, "The silver coin—".

Babette began to beat her drum more strongly and a curious hum, like bees droning, rose from it. Gaspard craned his neck and saw that a shallow brass plate fastened to the bottom of the drum vibrated at each beat.

"Will she never calve?" the peasant woman cried again. "Will her noble race die out? My charming Bluebell; her mother Gillyflower; her father Brutus and her brother Cassius,

all dead but she!" Choked with emotion she stopped her mouth with the back of her hand. In the silence, the simpleton said, "The silver coin I planted in the forest, will it grow to a tree of silver coins?"

The room burst into laughter, and when the echoes were still Père Fidèle had shuffled forward to stand nose to nose with the bird. He dropped a coin that wobbled on the table and pleaded, "Will my secret be found out?"

The bird opened its beak and said in a low, sweet, clear voice, "Yes." Gaspard, on tiptoe, could see its tongue vibrate.

"Will it really be found out?"

"Yes."

"Completely?"

"Yes."

"And soon?"

"Yes, sooner than you can imagine."

"Ah! At last!" Never taking his eyes from the bird, the old man shuffled backwards to his chimney corner.

"But what about my cow?" the peasant woman cried. "Is it possible that she should not calve? Consider how her horns sweep; how her tail swishes; how her ribs stir when she breathes, her brown and white spots like islands in the sea! Are all these to die out?"

The bird turned slowly to her and then, just as slowly, turned back again to the simpleton. "Your coin will sprout."

"Oh!" The simpleton fell to his knees, hands clasped. The room was so silent behind him that thc shoes on his trembling feet could be heard squeaking.

"It will bear fruit, but only every second year."

"Still . . ." the simpleton blinked.

"And then copper coins, not silver." The simpleton's round face fell, but the bird's voice was still clear and sweet as it added, "You didn't water it enough. You used the wrong kind of fertilizer."

"What should I use, then?" the simpleton cried, but the peasant woman broke in, "And my cow, my cow, my cow?"

The bird looked at her, then turned its head so that it was staring directly at Gaspard. The drum fell silent, and the bird sang:

Where will I hide, the strong thief said,
From the eye of the sun
And the tooth of the dog,
Where will I hide till darkness comes?

Crawl in beside me, the sapling sang,
I'll shade you, I'll shade you,
till sunlight is past,
Till the dog's bones are dry;
My limbs will give you a quiet home
Where you may rest when darkness comes.

It chirped a high note, then an arpeggio that descended two octaves, remounted to the first note with a chromatic scale, and covered its head with its wing. Silence grew around it, and Matthias solemnly stepped forward.

"Well, good people," he said, "the bird has answered two questions out of three and sung its song. It will speak no more this evening. No use in trying to force it. We know that Père Fidèle's secret will be found out, whatever it is, and that Simon's coin will bear fruit, though not exactly as he had planned. Perhaps someone here understands the song too. I never could. You all know the bird has spoken the truth, for it always does. How often do you hear two true things in one evening?"

"And my cow?" the peasant woman called, but her voice was tired now and was lost in the laughter and the tramping of feet as the crowd broke up.

"It was a very short performance," Gaspard said to the Duke. His mouth was dry. Somehow the performance, and especially the song, had disturbed him. He watched Matthias put the bird back in its cage and carry it from the room. "These people must be easily satisfied."

"Ah, that is Matthias's misfortune. These are easily satisfied. In such a low inn they are used to being cheated by mountebanks and it is rare that they get even as much satisfaction as they have had this evening; two answers for three questions is more than the bird usually gives, besides. In a large theatre—which is what Matthias aspired to once—the audience expects perfection and regularity. They would tear both him and his bird to feathers if it did not answer all questions. The word has gone round that they are unreliable; no impresario will touch them. I can tell you that Matthias is desperate. He has even asked me to sell him a family of dignified turtles that has lived in my garden for two hundred years. He thinks they can be trained to form geometrical patterns behind the bird to distract the public. This may be so, but none of my dependants has ever gone on the stage and at the moment I am free from the temptation to sell anything. But I worry about the bird. Matthias may link it up with a team of performing rats, or worse!"

The crowd was now thin enough for the Duke to put on his broad-brimmed hat, and he departed. Gaspard also returned to the stable where he had left his donkey, but, late as it was, he did not start for home. "You see, Anselm," he said, taking a seat on a new bale of hay, "Matthias is not a cruel person, but I am afraid he is narrow and selfish. He does not really value the bird highly enough, and this makes others set too low a value on it. This is not a bird for performing before great crowds, or even before small groups of nobles, much less in common inns. It is aristocratic itself, a noble creature. It must feel the vulgarity of such surroundings. No wonder it keeps silent. Wouldn't you keep quiet if I displayed you before a crowd and asked you to speak?" Anselm flipped one ear forward and back, but said nothing.

"And the bird's situation will become worse, too," Gaspard continued. "Soon it will have to share the stage with performing turtles, and who knows what else: ducks, rats, eels, even baboons? Matthias is not a man to be turned aside from a fixed idea. In such company it will talk less and less. It will even stop singing. Can't you see it caged in one corner of the platform, quite silent, the least part of a travelling animal show that no one but bored children and grandfathers will visit? No one will know it is there, and the children will stuff its cage with straw and scraps of old newspapers."

Gaspard pulled gently on Anselm's bridle and led the donkey from the stable, speaking to him again only when they were alone in the street. "Now, if I had the bird, you may be sure I would treat him quite differently. I wouldn't let such crowds see him, and pay him, and fill his lungs with smoke and wine fumes. No, I would let one person visit him at a time, two at most. I wouldn't carry him around on display, either: they would have to come to him." Anselm looked at him in surprise: they were not following the road by which they had entered town but a smaller one. "This way may be shorter," Gaspard explained.

"He would have a room to himself," Gaspard said. "His cage would stand in an alcove hung with red velvet. I would pull a cord when he wanted to rest, and a great velvet curtain would close him in. People who wanted to consult him would sit on a stool at his own level and would be warned to put each question only once. The price would be high; only wealthy people could afford it, but I would guarantee complete discretion and would watch from a distance or, better, plug my ears with wool." They turned into another narrow lane. "This may be the way," Gaspard said. After a minute's silence, marked only by the clip-clop of Anselm's hooves on the cobbles, he added, "But why should only rich people consult him? That would be selfish of me, and their problems might bore him. No, four days each month poor people could ask him questions free. But then, Anselm, some greedy folk might pretend to be poor to avoid paying." He thought this over as they turned downhill into yet another lane. "But of course!" he cried to his donkey. "The bird himself could detect impostors. If he can foretell the future, he will certainly know how much money people have now. We're silly to worry about him being cheated.

"Perhaps the red velvet chamber wouldn't suit him, though. He would feel too confined. A wide room, full of light and air, rather. His cage would be large enough to provide both sunlight and shade and for him to fly easily from one side to the other. I would strew the floor of the cage with bright shells and varnished wood and scraps of metal and cloth in case he wanted to build anything. I would hang bells on the side of the cage that he could ring with his beak or claw, rows of them tuned in chromatic scales, four full octaves. He could make his own melodies if he chose, or sing and accompany himself with the bells! If he did that, I wouldn't tell anyone but would listen all alone."

They emerged from the lane into a larger street and found themselves again facing the Golden Snail. "Well, we're a little out of our way," Gaspard said. "Only a little." He looked up at the stars twinkling through the cold, clear spring wind. "Possibly Matthias has simply left the cage in a shed or in the cellar with the vegetables. I am just going to make sure the bird is all right." He entered the inn by a side door. Anselm browsed silently in the narrow path between the street and the wall opposite the inn. The grass was tough and old, last summer's, hardly worth the trouble to eat, but he had cleaned off the length of a warehouse and two shop fronts before he heard his master return. An irregular bundle draped in an old black cloth sat on Gaspard's arm. At first he also tried to shield it under his coat, but it was much too large, and in a moment he grasped Anselm's bridle and stepped forth quickly, always keeping in the shadow. At the wider streets he waited to cross until tiny clouds had broken the sharp moonlight. The donkey's footsteps rang as clearly as ever, but Gaspard could not hear them for the beating of his heart. He whispered to his donkey, "He was in a little room by himself, Anselm. He might have grown cold." After another hundred steps Gaspard added, "Of course, there was a fire in the room, but it might have gone out."

During all this time the bundle on his arm hardly moved. He could feel the grasp of the bird's claws on his arm as it shifted to keep balance and the click of the light chain that he had fastened to his own wrist. "Don't think that I'm a thief, Anselm," the violin-maker said. "I saved the bird first. Is it right that I should have no part in it?" He waited for the donkey to answer, then spoke to Anselm's silence.

"Besides, I won't use it to become rich, as Matthias did. I could never bring myself to do that. The bird might think that I am a thief too. No, I will keep it with me and it can foretell the future to me." They entered a high, close alley that led to the open fields. Gaspard said, "No, that would be selfish too. I will let people who deserve to know the future ask him about it. That would be right, wouldn't it?" He moved a fold of the cloth and looked at the bundle, but no answer came. "Those to whom everything depended on knowing what will come," he explained. The bird was silent.

From behind them came the cough and whisper of a drum. Gaspard whirled around—the bird's claws tightened on his arm as he did so—and at the end of the alley saw the silhouette of Babette, still wearing her top hat. Her head and shoulders were motionless, but the light, steady drumbeat continued.

"Well, it's all over," Gaspard said to the bird. "You might as well breathe, too. You can call for help

now." He pulled the cloth off the bird's head. But the bird did not call out. It spoke in a calm voice, apparently to Babette: "Did I ever tell you about the foolish little black bat? It loved the fields and sunlight so much that it gathered flowers to light its cage. It filled all the crannies with golden buttercups and fanned them with its wings to make them glow." The bird chuckled. "Of course, they all faded."

Gaspard shivered. When it became clear that neither Babette nor the bird was going to cry out, he continued out of town, marching to the light beat of Babette's drum that faded behind them as they left her standing there. They walked along quite openly, but as they approached the bridge, Gaspard led Anselm off the path and downhill through the sparse bush to the riverbed. High above them the toll bridge stretched, a bar across the sky. They crossed the river on flat stones laced with black water that rushed by with a curious sucking sound and climbed the other side by a dim path that led back to the road.

The bird's beak flashed in the moonlight, though its eyes were in shadow. "The dog might have leaped at you if we had tried to pass the bridge so late," Gaspard said. "No, that wouldn't have happened," he added. "You know I was afraid that Matthias's cousin would be awake or that you would call for help as we crossed the bridge. But you could call for help now. They could still hear you in the toll house." The bird moved its beak up and down, and was silent.

They turned in to the path that led to the violin-maker's hut. "We are going to my home," Gaspard said. "It seems strange that for all the times I have seen you—even though they were only a few times—you have not visited me till now." They walked through the pine forest. The donkey and the violin-maker with the bird on his arm made tall, striding shadows in the moonlight between the still, endless shadows of the trees.

"No one saw me take you," Gaspard said, "only Babette. Still, we should leave. I'll pack my tools and my violins and some pots and pans, and some clothes, and load them on Anselm's back; there is not so much as to weigh him down; besides, he is very strong. We will find some other place to live, some other cabin in the forest. We can go to the mountains where the smugglers live and where everyone keeps out of his neighbour's business, or even farther away, to Russia, or Africa, or the New World. A good violin-maker can always earn a living. Where would you like to go?" The bird did not answer.

They entered Gaspard's hut. He lit a lamp, and unwound the bird's chain from his own wrist and attached it to a nail on his work-bench. "That will have to do until I find you some place that is more comfortable," he said. He looked at the bird, within touching distance now, and in a clear light. How it had changed! All the light wisps of down he had once seen at the edge of the wings and along the back of the neck were gone. The feathers lay on each other as smoothly as ripples of sand on a beach and seemed to slide over one another as the wing trembled. Only at the rear edge of the wing—now that the bird had negligently stretched it out a little—was the smoothness broken by a few protruding feathers of dark gold in which Gaspard could dimly see his own face reflected. He could sense the play of muscles under the wing and see the powerful swell of the breast. The bill was hooked like a golden scimitar, which the bird now polished more brightly by stroking it up and down on the underside of its wing.

"This is where I work." Gaspard pointed to the bench. He did not expect the bird to answer, nor did it, but he continued. "There are all my tools. I use these fine saws to cut out the patterns for violins and those planes and this draw-knife to shave the wood thin. Then I must use many chisels for gouging out the wood to the right thickness and for making the scrolls. I use these tiny ones for inlaid work." He held up a spruce shaving, and the bird touched it with the tip of one claw. "Spruce for the belly," Gaspard said, "maple for the back and ribs and for the neck and scrolls. You see how scrolls are usually carved." He pointed to one. "But anything may be carved there: lions, or birds, or fishes, or men's heads. If you wish, I will keep you chained to my bench and you can watch me work. I would value your opinion." The bird dug the tip of a claw, effortlessly, into the hard wood of the bench. These powerful curved claws seemed proper for clutching a granite boulder, Gaspard thought, but awkward and out of place on the flat bench-top. "I will find you a rock to stand on," he said quickly.

"The wood for violins must be properly seasoned. I have pieces in my shed that are over ten years old, quite dry. We will have to take them with us when we move. I will make several trips with Anselm. But if we go too far away we will have to leave the wood behind, all but some really choice pieces. But I can find well-seasoned wood in old houses they are tearing down. You would be amazed at the wonderful old spruce beams hidden away behind the trashy cornices, and the solid maple panelling, too. The wood is old and scarred, no one wants it, and you can buy it for a song. Then, a few strokes of the plane and the clear, straight grain shines through. The surface seems to invite you to cut it into beautiful shapes." The bird, still silent, looked at Gaspard calmly, with complete understanding.

"Well," Gaspard said, "then I will let you go." He lifted the chain which was fastened to a thin ring around the bird's ankle. It held out its foot stiffly, and with a pair of pincers, Gaspard cut the ring in two places. The bird shook this foot, then the other; then it bent its knees and strongly, though clumsily, launched itself. It flew across the room, turned at the wall without touching it, and then, swiftly flapping its wide wings, settled so gently on the cord crossing the room that the violins hanging from it barely danced. "I knew how to fly, of course, in theory," it remarked, "but I wasn't really sure I could until I had tried it. It's quite easy."

"Will you fly away now?" Gaspard asked.

"Soon. We live very high in the air and only settle on mountain tops. I was beginning to feel dull and heavy here. Of course, I couldn't live with you or with any human being. But since you let me go, I can talk with you a little. And let me tell you," it added, "now that I'm free and can talk directly, what a relief to do so without all those riddles!" The bird's eyes took on a shrewd, pedantic look. "Poetry and parables are all very well when you're a captive and have to hide your meaning, or when you're feeling very elated. So I understand: I never felt elated till now. But for the ordinary business of life, give me direct prose!"

The bird flew from the cord—this time the hanging violins did rattle together—and glided back to the work-bench.

"Do you really know everything?" Gaspard asked.

"Most things. Of course, we reason out some by first principles."

"What would have happened to you if I hadn't rescued you from the tower?"

"Oh, I would have been killed. There was one great hairy fellow below; his thick boot would have crushed my skull. Young as I was, I could understand what might happen if I had fallen to the ground in that crowd."

Gaspard shook his head. "You must have been frightened."

"A little, because I didn't know if you would come in time."

"But I did come. Well then, if I had kept you, would you have grown?"

The bird hesitated. "That isn't certain. Everything isn't always certain, you know; there is always some sense in making a choice. But I was very young, my digestion was delicate, even Matthias had one or two bad nights with me. You wouldn't believe how patient he was!"

"Did you grow fond of him?"

"Naturally. We have emotions too, especially when we are young. But my success had gone to his head. He was beginning to value me only for the fame and wealth I brought him and there was less and less of that. Still, he would never have set me free. You did that."

The bird touched Gaspard's finger lightly with its claw. "I never had anyone to talk to. They fought over everything I said as if it were a bank-note. If I had happened to mention that the mice between the walls were complaining of the cold, they would have smoked them out. I couldn't even say that my feathers itched without someone writing it down in a little book. And my feathers did itch. They felt full of smoke and dull thoughts. How I longed to be free, flying in the thin air! I will have to fly a long time without ever touching ground to get my feathers clean."

The bird began to fold and unfold its wings with a crisp, rustling sound and to rock back and forth. Gaspard asked, "Are there many of you?"

PANTON

"Only a very few, but we live a long time. The others were terrified to see me captured. They flew high above, almost out of your sight, and called to me and taught me. When we speak to each other our voices are so high that no one else can hear them."

"But how did you come to be on the angel's wing where I found you?"

"We build our nests on clouds, but my mother was old and had become careless. The cloud she chose was soft and fluffy but not strong enough; it flew low the night I hatched and dissolved into mist against the church wall and left me there."

The bird began to walk up and down the work-bench, leaving faint tracks in the shavings. Its brow wrinkled. "Before I go—since you are the only person who ever spoke to me without making a request, though you would have been most justified in asking—I will tell you something you may want to know. You should go to the mountains, high in the mountains, in early spring, it must be before all the snow melts, and look among the birch roots for a plant a few inches high with smooth green bark and five spiky leaves at its crown. You'll know it when you see it. Dry it and cut it into thin strips. Inlay these in the belly of your violins, just below the bridge. This is one way to make violins that sing with a human voice, if you want to."

The bird tapped the window with its claw and waited, a little impatiently, till Gaspard swung back the pane and the shutter. Night had passed; a thin, chill dawn air entered the room. The bird hopped to the sill and without another word flapped off through the forest, heavily at first, but steadily mounting higher and higher. The beat of its wings still echoed among the pine trees after it was out of sight, and by leaning over the bench and out the window Gaspard could see it rising past the highest trees, glowing in the sunrise, and up through the pale dawn air, so clear that the bird seemed suspended there as a dot that shrank little by little till the trailing edge of a cloud casually erased it.

CHAPTER SEVEN

FOR MANY YEARS afterwards people still spoke of Matthias's wonderful bird. The tales of its appearance and its power became more and more fabulous. These stories described more than its golden feathers and golden claws: the bird's eyes were also said to give off light in a dark room and its beak to split rocks. It was reported that not only could it predict future events but it could change their course. No one suspected that Gaspard had taken it, and Babette never told. Some said it was gypsies; others that the bird had freed itself, biting through its chain and the bars of its cage like paper; yet others that the bird had been smuggled away by the servants of one of the lords who had seen it, and that this lord now kept it in a locked room in his castle, growing daily in wisdom and power through its help. In lonely caves in the hills shrines to the bird appeared— as other shrines appeared to the sun and the moon and the wind—crude drawings in red and gold on flat rocks, with little offerings of fruit or dried corn or wild flowers.

Matthias did not speak at first of his disappointment at losing his bird, but he did not take up his plan of exhibiting other animals.

Some profits still remained to him and he built a small inn near the toll bridge. He called it The Golden Bird and hung a picture of the head of a fierce golden eagle over the door. This once lonely spot became full of gay and busy travellers, for, as a landlord, Matthias put aside some of the dignity he had felt called on to assume as toll-keeper. He was always ready to exchange stories about the bird he had once owned, though he permitted none of the more far-fetched tales to pass his chimney corner without correction. He also took care that his guests' glasses were full and their rooms well aired. He often said, "Even though I lost the bird, he did me some good in return for my bringing him up. He brought me out into the world again and showed me the pleasures of a more sociable life."

Babette grew much calmer and only saw visions at Easter time. She began to help her husband in the inn. All the countryside called her "Aunt Babette". It was forgotten that she had once been thought mad, and her cooking and her cheerful smile drew customers to the Golden Bird.

Matthias's second cousin still watched the toll bridge. In time this cousin married, and a flock of cheerful, sleepy-eyed children with hairy ears grew up around him, swinging on the toll gate, fishing in the steam, and playing on the back of the great dog, Wagram, who on sunny days lay in the dust before the inn, his nose pointing at the bridge.

Gaspard went to the mountains early every spring to search for the plant with five spiky leaves in its crown. They were difficult to find. He recognized one the first time he saw it, but he could not find more than two or three in a year, enough for half a dozen violins. Sometimes he would pass a week in the mountains before he found even one plant. After he had made the violins as the bird had told him and had heard them sing, he carried them to Toulouse, and later to Paris, to sell. Each one sounded as if a human soul were imprisoned in the wood, not crying for release but perfectly content to be there. Gaspard would play each violin for many hours at a time before he sold it, and his face took on a very puzzled expression, as if he could not quite make out what the voice was saying.

The violins commanded high prices. In time Gaspard became concerned about all the money and the valuable violins he was keeping in his lonely cabin and bought a workshop on the outskirts of Toulouse, where his donkey could graze and amble in the fields. But the pressures of business worried him; his uncertainty whether he would find the plant again the following spring made him anxious and his face took on a drawn, peaked look. The days he spent each spring in the cold mountain rains and wet snow damaged his health. He became bent and his bones hurt when he walked, but he continued climbing into the mountains as long as he was able, supporting himself by leaning on Anselm's back. Later, he let the donkey, who never seemed to grow older, carry him up all the hills and he even trained Anselm to pluck the plant with his teeth.

CHAPTER EIGHT

WE KNOW TODAY how Gaspard's violins sounded only through reading critics of the time and a few private letters. Famous violinists used these instruments. Sarasate would play nothing else in the smaller towns of southern Spain, though for the more sophisticated audiences in Madrid and Barcelona he used his Stradivarius. Ysaye once played one of Gaspard's violins before the Czar of Russia. The sound of the violins was described as that of a young girl singing at dawn, or of a child calling for its mother. The best-known violin of all, the so-called "Lyrebird", had a voice that reminded the critic who described it of a sage standing in a desert, singing into the wind all the truths of life. But we must remember that this was a time of fine phrases, when even critics exaggerated.

As the violins grew older their human voices gradually disappeared. They went, not as other human voices do, first becoming hoarse or cracked or strident, but in a more kindly way, fading little by little, so that fifty years after a violin was made no trace of the human voice remained, only a clear, smooth tone like water flowing over polished rocks. They still respond eagerly to the bow and, though they are not brilliant enough for the great soloists, they are prized for their tranquil spirit and their elegant, beautiful construction. In making all the violins in which he inlaid bits of wood from the plant of the high mountains, Gaspard put more skill and love than he would have ever thought possible, and these are still evident when you hold one of his violins in your hand. You cannot mistake them for the violins of another maker: on the side of each scroll, so that the player can touch it gently with his forefinger, Gaspard carved a small bird with outstretched wings. It is carved in such spirit and detail that individual feathers are visible, and the bird always seems to be on the point of taking flight.

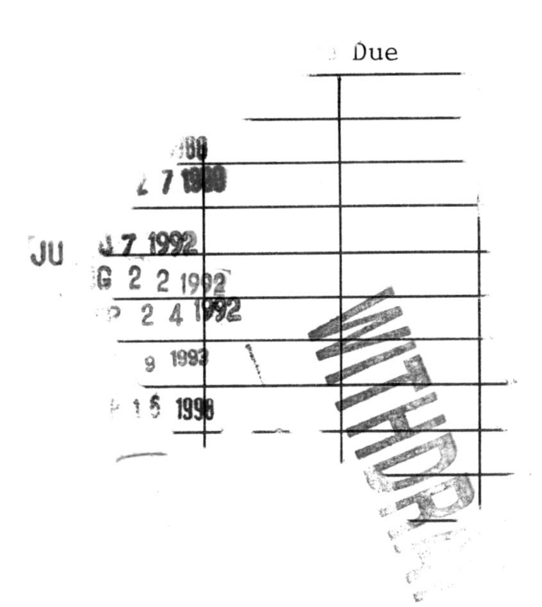
Due